BIG BOYS
GO POTTY

No More Diapers!

Peter's New Potty

WRITTEN AND ILLUSTRATED BY
Marianne Richmond

sourcebooks
jabberwocky

Published by Sourcebooks Jabberwocky, an imprint of
Sourcebooks, Inc.
P.O. Box 4410, Naperville, Illinois 60567-4410
(630) 961-3900
Fax: (630) 961-2168
www.jabberwockykids.com

Library of Congress Cataloging-in-Publication data is on
file with the publisher.

Source of Production: Leo Paper, Heshan City,
Guangdong Province, China
Date of Production: January 2012
Run Number: 16835

Printed and bound in China.
LEO 10 9 8 7 6 5 4 3 2

**Also available from author & illustrator
Marianne Richmond:**

The Gift of an Angel
The Gift of a Memory
Hooray for You!
The Gifts of Being Grand
I Love You So…
Dear Daughter
Dear Son
Dear Granddaughter
Dear Grandson
Dear Mom
My Shoes Take Me Where I Want to Go
Happy Birthday to You!
I Love You So Much…
You Are My Wish Come True
Big Sister
Big Brother
If I Could Keep You Little
The Night Night Book
Beautiful Brown Eyes
Beautiful Blue Eyes
I Wished for You, an adoption story
I Believe in You
I'm Not Tired Yet!
Daddy Loves Me!
Mama Loves Me!
Grandpa Loves Me!
Grandma Loves Me!
Pink Wiggly Pig

Find more heartfelt books and
beautiful gifts for all occasions at
www.mariannerichmond.com

Hi, my name is Daniel, and
this is my friend, Lion.

I'm a big boy now.
I can swing real high.

I can talk to Lion.

I can play blocks with Mommy and Daddy.
What kind of big boy things can you do?

I still wear diapers though.

Big boys use the potty
to go pee pee and poop.
Do you?

Mommy and Daddy are so excited to give me my very own potty because it's the right size for me!

Lion and I sit on
the potty and read
books but no pee
or poop happens.

Then it happens when
it isn't supposed to!

My daddy says accidents
are part of learning and
that they are okay!

Mommy gives me a
sticker every time
I remember to use
the potty.

I get better the
more I practice.
You will, too!

Finally, I do it
all by myself!

I use the right amount of toilet paper.
Mommy and Daddy say a few pieces are enough!

Too much paper is
bad for the potty.

I flush and watch
my pee pee and
poop go bye-bye!

I wash my hands
with soap and water
and dry them with
a towel.

Now I use the potty
every time I have to
go pee pee or poop.

I like being dry and
cozy more than being
wet and messy.

Mommy and Lion and I
went shopping for big boy
underwear with trains on it.

Mommy and Daddy
are so proud of me.

I am proud of me, too!

I like being a big boy. Do you?

About the Author

Marianne Richmond is the bestselling author and illustrator of numerous beautiful books for parents and children to share. She creates emotional and thoughtful stories that children of any age will appreciate now and forever.